Bear S

Written by Adam and Charlotte Guillain

One snowy day, Tess, Finn and their friends were helping at the wildlife park.

They were digging snow away from
the footpath when a fresh flurry of snowflakes
swirled around them.

A blizzard lifted the friends off their feet and they closed their eyes. When they landed, they were gazing at a glistening white landscape.

"We're in the Arctic!" cried Finn, pointing at an Arctic fox. They followed the little white animal across the snow.

Rav spotted something moving up ahead. The fox saw it too, and froze. Then the fox darted into a hole and vanished.

The friends walked across the snow and found some polar bear cubs.

They're so cute!

"Play with us!" shouted one of the bears, sliding down the icy slope.

Tess laughed and copied the cub.

"Let's play hide and seek next!" said Finn.

"Our mum will be back soon," said the biggest cub. "We should go home."

"Let's all hide and surprise her!" said the smallest cub. The friends squeezed through the hole into the bears' den.

"It's cosy in here!" whispered Asha.

"Where's your mum been?" asked Rav.
"Hunting for food!" said the biggest cub.
"I'm hungry!"

"I can hear her coming," whispered
the smallest cub. "Let's all jump out and roar
when she comes in!"

They waited … and waited …

The mother bear's nose appeared at the hole.

"Now!" cried the bear cubs.

"ROAR!" shouted the friends.

The mother bear jumped back and stared.

"*I* didn't find any food," she said. "But what have *you* found?" She sniffed inside and grinned.

Tess gulped. "I think we might be lunch if we don't get out of here!" she whispered.

These are our new friends, Mum!

The mother bear just licked her lips.

Asha, Rav, Tess and Finn looked at each other worriedly. "How are we going to escape?" whispered Asha.

Rav thought quickly. "Um, we're playing hide and seek," he said. "Close your eyes and count to ten."

One … two …

As soon as the polar bears shut their eyes, Rav grabbed his friends and they ran out of the den.

Five … six …

"That was close!" gasped Finn as a blizzard lifted them upwards.

"We're going home," said Asha.

"Just in time!" laughed Finn.

Nine … ten!

Talk about the story

Answer the questions:

1 Where did the friends travel to in the story?

2 How many polar bear cubs were there?

3 Why did Tess say, "I think we might be lunch if we don't get out of here!"?

4 How did Rav trick the polar bears?

5 How would you have escaped from the polar bears?

6 Have you ever been somewhere very cold? Did you have to wear special clothes?

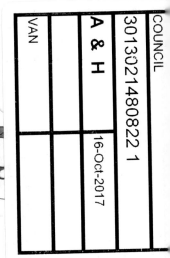

Can you retell the story in your own words?